Jabber Jabber

ISBN 979-8-88851-325-5 (Paperback)
ISBN 979-8-88851-327-9 (Hardcover)
ISBN 979-8-88851-326-2 (Digital)

Covenant Books
11661 Hwy 707
Murrells Inlet, SC 29576
www.covenantbooks.com

Jabber Jabber

BY JAMES LUTTRELL

ILLUSTRATIONS BY KENT CLARK

LUKE AND LILLY LIVED WITH THEIR MOTHER AND FATHER. THEIR HOUSE WAS IN A CLEARING ON THE EDGE OF THE JUNGLE. BESIDES THE FAMILY, THEY HAD A PET MONKEY THAT LIVED WITH THEM. JABBER JABBER WAS HIS NAME BECAUSE OF HIS CONSTANT CHATTER!

THEY WERE VERY HAPPY!

ONE DAY, LUKE, LILLY, AND JABBER JABBER WERE PLAYING IN THE YARD. THEY WERE LAUGHING AT JABBER JABBER AS HE DID HIS ANTICS.

SUDDENLY, JABBER JABBER RAN INTO THE THICK JUNGLE, SWINGING FROM TREE TO TREE. LUKE AND LILLY BEGAN CALLING AND RUNNING AFTER HIM. THEY HAD BEEN TOLD NOT TO GO INTO THE JUNGLE, BUT THEY CONTINUED TO FOLLOW JABBER JABBER AS HE WENT DEEPER INTO THE JUNGLE WHERE WILD ANIMALS LIVED.

ON AND ON, DEEPER AND DEEPER THEY WENT, FOLLOWING AFTER THE MONKEY, CALLING OUT TO HIM AS THEY RAN.

FINALLY, THEY CAME TO A SMALL OPENING, AND THERE WAS JABBER JABBER.

HE WAS SITTING UNDER A LARGE BANANA TREE.

LUKE AND LILLY LAUGHED AT HIM SITTING THERE UNDER THE BANANA TREE,
A BANANA IN EACH HAND. HE WAS EATING THEM AS FAST AS HE COULD. THEY
BEGAN EATING BANANAS TOO. THEY ATE UNTIL THEY COULDN'T EAT MORE.

IT WAS TIME TO GO BACK HOME. THEY EACH HAD BUNCHES
OF BANANAS TO CARRY WITH THEM.

THEY WERE A LONG WAY FROM HOME.

SUDDENLY, A GIANT GORILLA STEPPED INTO THE PATH. THEY FROZE WITH FEAR. THE GORILLA LOOKED FIERCE! THE GORILLA LOOKED DOWN AT LUKE. HE LOOKED DOWN AT THE BUNCHES OF BANANAS LUKE WAS CARRYING. LUKE HANDED HIM A BANANA. THE GORILLA TOOK IT AND ATE IT.

ONE BY ONE, LUKE HANDED HIM HIS BANANAS, UNTIL THEY WERE ALL GONE.

ONE BY ONE, LILLY HANDED THE GORILLA HER BANANAS, UNTIL THEY WERE ALL GONE.

ONE BY ONE, JABBER JABBER HANDED HIM HIS BANANAS, UNTIL THEY WERE ALL GONE.

FULL OF BANANAS, THE GORILLA LAY DOWN AND WENT TO SLEEP.

QUIETLY, LUKE, LILLY, AND JABBER JABBER CREPT AROUND THE LARGE, SLEEPING GORILLA.

RUNNING AS FAST AS THEY COULD, THEY SOON SAW THEIR HOME
IN THE CLEARING AT THE EDGE OF THE JUNGLE.

THEY WERE SO GLAD TO BE HOME! LUKE AND LILLY BEGAN
PLAYING AND LAUGHING AT JABBER JABBER.

THEY NEVER WENT INTO THE JUNGLE AGAIN.

THEY WERE HAPPY!

THE END.

ABOUT THE AUTHOR

JAMES LUTTRELL WAS BORN IN HARDEMAN COUNTY, TENNESSEE. HE WAS RAISED ON A SMALL FARM AT A TIME FAMILY FARMS WERE ABUNDANT. HE IS MARRIED AND THE FATHER OF THREE CHILDREN. HE WORKED VARIOUS JOBS. JAMES HAS HAD A LOVE FOR HORSES SINCE HE WAS A CHILD, AND THAT'S HOW HE DECIDED ON THE OCCUPATION OF A FARRIER. THAT BECAME HIS LIFE WORK. EVENTUALLY, STORIES TOLD TO HIS CHILDREN WERE WRITTEN DOWN. JABBER JABBER IS ONE OF THESE STORIES.